CLASSIC COLLECTION

PERSEUS
~ AND ~
MEDUSA

ADAPTED BY SAVIOUR PIROTTA · ILLUSTRATED BY MIKE LOVE

QED Publishing

The Baby in the Chest

It was getting dark and chilly. Dictys the fisherman was dragging his boat on to the sandy beach. It had been a long day and his wicker baskets were full of fish; there was enough to eat for the next few days, and perhaps some to sell too.

Out of the corner of his eye, Dictys saw something large floating along the line of the shore. For a moment he thought it was some plank of wood from a wrecked ship. Then, moving closer, he realized it was a large wooden chest, bobbing on the tide. Its lid was carved all over with snakes and sirens and there was a big metal hoop, a handle, at either end.

He grabbed one of the hoops and dragged the chest ashore. Then, using his oar, he forced the lid open. Inside was a woman, curled up like a baby in a cradle. She was obviously rich; her gown was made of beautiful blue-dyed linen. There was a gold necklace round her neck and bangles on her wrists. Dictys held the back of his hand against her lips. She was breathing softly, alive but asleep.

Clasped in the sleeping woman's arms was a bundle. As Dictys watched, it twitched ever so slightly. He pulled it gently out of the woman's grasp and unwrapped it. The covering fell to reveal a baby, dressed in fine robes. It was sound asleep but, disturbed by Dictys' fumbling, it woke up and let out an ear-piercing howl…

"Give that little child here," said Dictys' wife Clymene, as he approached their little hut with the bawling baby.

She took the child in her arms and rocked him gently, soothing him to sleep. Dictys returned to the wooden chest and, lifting the sleeping woman out of it, carried her gently to his house.

When she woke up, she explained to Dictys and Clymene, "I am Queen Danae, and this is my son, Perseus. The oracle told my father, King Acrisius of Argos, that his own grandson would grow up to kill him and steal his throne. So he had us locked in a chest and thrown into the sea, hoping we would drown or starve to death. But Zeus seems to be protecting us, for here we are, rescued and safe."

Dictys told Danae they were on the island of Seriphos. "We don't have much, as you can see," said Clymene, gesturing at the simple furnishings in the hut, "but you and your son are welcome to live with us. Dictys catches enough fish in the summer to feed all of us and in winter we harvest wheat to make the best bread on the island."

Soon Danae and Perseus had settled into their new life. Danae made herself useful, weaving rugs and shawls, which she and Clymene sold at the market. As a queen she had been taught how to sew the most delicate embroidery and her shawls always fetched a good price.

A Royal Invitation

Now Dictys might have been a poor fisherman but his brother, Polydectes, was the king of Seriphos. News of Danae's arrival didn't take long to travel round the island and soon Polydectes came to pay his brother a rare visit.

The moment the king set his eyes on Danae, he wanted her for his wife. She refused, claiming her first duty was to look after her son. Polydectes was not used to having his demands turned down. He threatened to make Danae his queen by force. She had, after all, been found in a chest on the shore – and anything that washed up on Seriphos from the sea was, by rights, the king's property.

"Perhaps," said Danae as a comprimise, "I will reconsider your kind proposal when my son grows up."

But the years passed and Danae did not change her mind. Polydectes kept sending her gifts; she always sent them back.

Perseus grew into a tall, handsome, strong young man.

"Do not worry, mother," he would say every time Polydectes came to call. "I will protect you from any suitor that approaches you."

Now, it seemed, Polydectes had finally given up on the idea of marrying Danae. A messenger from the palace arrived to announce a royal wedding.

"The king Polydectes is to wed Hippodameia, daughter of the king of Pisa. All the men on the island are invited to the king's banquet before the wedding, and to bring with them the traditional marriage gift of a horse."

Bring Me the Head of Medusa

"Sire, I have no horse to give."

Perseus was standing in front of Polydectes in the palace courtyard. The banquet was about to start. A delicious smell of roast boar and lamb hung in the air.

Everyone but Perseus had brought the king a horse, the symbol of a successful marriage with many children to come.

"No horse?" gasped the king's attendant at Perseus. "It is a grave offence to attend the king's banquet without presenting your gift. I believe the punishment for such an outrage is exile…"

"But I have no horse of my own to give," argued Perseus, "and no money to buy one. I thought it would be even worse if I refused the king's invitation."

The king raised his hand to silence the argument. A mysterious smile was playing on his lips, for the whole banquet was a charade, a trick. Polydectes had no intention of marrying Hippodameia. He wanted to marry Danae, and he'd hatched a plot to get rid of Perseus.

"I am sure he did not mean to offend," he said to his attendant.

"On the contrary," cut in Perseus. "I wanted to pay my respects."

Polydectes smiled. "And if you had the money, young man, what gift would you bring me?'"

"Anything. Ask and I will fetch it," insisted Perseus.

"Well," said the king, "in that case, I would like you to fetch me the head of Medusa!"

Gifts from the Gods

Medusa was a gorgon, a monster. Legend had it that she had poisonous snakes on her head instead of hair. Her body was covered in scales so thick no spear or arrow could pierce them. She had bronze claws, and could fly about on golden wings. Her mouth was full of sharp teeth. Her tongue was a venomous snake too. Come close enough, and it would bite you. Only no one ever came close enough to be killed by Medusa's snake. Like her two sisters, Stheno and Euryale, the gorgon had a weapon no one could survive. Her eyes could turn people to stone.

Not that Perseus was in any danger of being turned to stone by Medusa just yet. He had to find her first, and no one in the world seemed to know where she and the other two gorgons lived!

Returning home to Dictys, Perseus stood talking to his mother. She was sat at her loom, spinning.

"Oh, my son, I fear the king has played a cruel trick on you," said Danae. "He wants you out of the way so 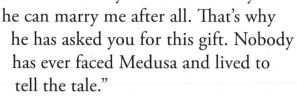 he can marry me after all. That's why he has asked you for this gift. Nobody has ever faced Medusa and lived to tell the tale."

"Then I will make sure to bring him back the gorgon's head," replied Perseus. "Mother, he will regret playing tricks on me."

10

"You must pray to the gods for counsel," added Clymene from her own loom on the porch.

"Yes," said Perseus, "I shall pray to Athena. It is said Medusa was once a beautiful woman but the goddess turned her into a hideous gorgon for offering a sick lamb in her temple."

He strode out to the orchard behind Dictys' hut. It was a clear night. A full moon was shining, turning the leaves on the trees a silver colour. Suddenly a breeze swept through the orchard, scattering leaves on the night air. Somewhere an owl hooted.

"Who walks among the sacred trees at this bewitching hour?" called a voice from behind a gnarled olive tree, and a woman stepped out in Perseus' path.

"It is I, Perseus."

The owl fluttered down from the branches of the tree and settled on the woman's shoulder. Its eyes blinked at Perseus. The woman smiled kindly. "Do not be alarmed, Perseus," she said. "I am Athena. Your mother has prayed that I help you. As you know, I loathe Medusa and would have slain her with my own hands had Zeus not forbidden it. So here is something to help you destroy her for me."

Athena held out a shield, round as the full moon. "When you approach the gorgon, do not look her directly in the eyes," she warned, "or you will be turned to stone. Instead, look at her reflection in this."

As she spoke, a second person joined her. He too was tall, and carried a lyre that seemed to glow in the moonlight. There was another fluttering of wings in the branches of the olive tree and a rooster settled on the man's shoulder.

"I am the god Hermes," he said. "Dictys the fisherman offered a sacrifice to me that I might help you."

He held out a dagger in a curved sheath. "Take this. The blade is carved from adamant. It is the only metal that can pierce a gorgon's scales."

"I thank you both," said Perseus. He strapped the dagger to his leather belt and hung Athena's shield from his right arm. "But where shall I find the dreaded gorgons?" asked Perseus.

"Ah, only the nymphs of the underworld know that, and they can give you gifts to help you on your quest," replied Athena.

"Where shall I find the nymphs of the underworld?"

"Ask the grey women, the sisters of the gorgons. They'll know," answered Hermes.

Perseus looked from one god to the other. He felt helpless. Every question was answered with a riddle. Athena laughed, and the owl hooted loudly.

Hermes held out his hands and a pair of sandals appeared in them. They glittered in the moonlight, little wings fluttering at the straps.

"Put these on, Perseus. They will take you wherever you ask them."

The Grey Sisters

"Sandals, take me to the grey women," commanded Perseus and a moment later the wings started fluttering against his ankles. He rose swiftly in the air. The ground below him fell away, the vineyards and olive groves getting smaller and smaller until they resembled a delicate pattern on a blanket.

Then the clouds drew a veil under his feet and he found himself in a heavenly realm, with nothing above but the cobalt blue of the sky. When the clouds parted again he noticed that the landscape below him had changed. He landed in a deep valley, a gorge. It was completely silent, as if the whole world were dead. He peered around him and saw the outlines of leafless trees against the moonlight. Then he heard, very faintly, the sound of crows cawing.

He climbed one of the dead trees and looked around. In the distance he could see a faint light. He strode across the hard stony ground towards it. The light turned out to be firelight streaming out of a stone hut with a sloping roof, its chimney belching thick smoke.

As Perseus approached, a dark figure hobbled to the open doorway. It stood there framed in the light, a bent old woman with a hump on her back.

"Who comes near?"

"It is I," replied Perseus, "a weary traveller in search of advice from the three wise women they call the grey sisters."

A second figure hobbled to the doorway.

"Do I hear the voice of a man, Deino?"

The first woman nodded fiercely. She was looking Perseus up and down with one glassy eye. Her other eye socket was empty, a dark hole in a wizened face.

"Aye, he is handsome indeed, Enyo."

The second woman cackled with laughter. Coming closer, Perseus realized she couldn't see him at all. Both her eye sockets were empty.

"Let me see him for myself, sister," she begged. "I haven't laid eyes on a handsome hero for many a year."

A third woman, just as bent and shrivelled as the first two, appeared at the door. "Deino, Enyo, what be this fuss about?"

She cocked her head to one side, her hairy chin quivering, and Perseus could see she too had no eyes.

"A man is at our door, dear sister Pemphredo," replied Deino.

"He seeks our advice," added Enyo.

"What advice can we give a stranger?" cried Pemphredo.

"I want to know," said Perseus, "where to find the nymphs of the underworld, so that I can destroy Medusa."

The three women gasped all together. Deino's one eye blinked rapidly.

"That," snapped Pemphredo, "is a secret we will never divulge. Medusa might turn us to stone."

"No," laughed Deino. "We shall never tell you that."

"Never in a million years," added Enyo.

The three sisters grinned, showing toothless gums except for Pemphredo, who had one yellow tooth. Then Enyo purred like a cat.

"But sisters, he must be a hero indeed if he dares search for the gorgons. Let me have a look at him."

She held out a bony hand to Deino. "Come on, sister, hand the eye over. It is only fair."

Pemphredo put out her hand too, wiggling long, bony fingers. "Give it to me first, Deino. I am the oldest."

"You already have the tooth, Pemphredo," complained Enyo. "You've been chewing meat all morning. Let me use the eye first. It is only fair."

Deino cackled with laughter again. "I think I shall keep it a little longer."

"Oh, you cruel beast," hissed Enyo. "Hand it over."

"Very well," said Deino. "But in return I must keep the tooth all through dinner tonight." She grinned at Perseus, "You see, sir, we have only one eye and one tooth between us. It is very trying, sharing them round, especially when you have sisters as greedy as mine."

"Greed," said Perseus, "does no one any good." He watched closely as Deino raised her fingers to her face and plucked out the eye. She handed it to Enyo who placed it in one of her eye sockets.

"My," said Enyo, goggling at Perseus, "the young warrior is handsome indeed."

"Now let me see him," cried Pemphredo, keen to see the handsome stranger.

"Here you are, sister," said Enyo. She removed the eye, holding it out carefully towards Pemphredo. Perseus darted forward and snatched it out of her hand.

"That was rude of you, sister," cried Enyo.

"That wasn't Pemphredo," said Perseus, "that was me."

The three women gasped. "You took it?"

"Thief!"

"Give it back."

"I'll return it once you tell me where the nymphs live," he retorted.

The women gasped in horror and grabbed each other for support. They knew Perseus had them cornered. Without the eye, all three of them were doomed to a life of eternal darkness.

"Tell him," cried Enyo to Pemphredo. "Even if he finds the gorgons, he will never live to tell the tale."

Pemphredo pointed a bony finger at the spot where she thought Perseus was standing. "You will find the nymphs by the River Styx in the underworld, which is right at the very end of the world itself," she cried. "Now give us back our eye and be gone."

"Thank you," laughed Perseus. "But I would learn some kindness if I were you. Cruelty never pays."

He let the eyeball drop, rolling along the dirty ground. The women shrieked, and began to search blindly for it.

"You wicked mortal. The gorgons will destroy you…"

Perseus rose up in the air on his sandals. He didn't have time to listen to their threats; he had some nymphs to find.

On the Banks of the River

The wild terrain quickly disappeared from view, the grey sisters shrinking until they could be seen no more. The mist closed around Perseus again and he could see nothing but the hazy outline of the moon far above. He travelled for a long time, while the world seemed to be asleep, wrapped in a blanket of silence.

Then he felt himself falling gently, the wings on the sandals beating against his ankles. At last he felt solid ground under his feet. There was no moon or stars above and he realized he was somewhere underground. Had he reached the underworld?

Perseus stood still and listened out for any noise. He could hear nothing but the splash of water nearby. Before long his eyes got used to the darkness and he could make out the outlines of huge, jagged rocks all around him. They had tall, old trees growing out of the top of them. It was hot and airless.

"Welcome, stranger."

"Yes, welcome. It has been a long time since we last saw a mortal."

"Yes, a very long time. Welcome!"

The voices were whispers, carried on the warm breeze, but they made him jump just the same.

"Where are you?" asked Perseus.

"We are standing on the banks of the river. It is cooler here. You need to stay close to the water in this airless heat. Come closer, come closer, stranger, and you will see us."

Perseus approached the river and there they were, three young maidens, their robes made of water plants and pearls. They were standing in the cool water.

"Such a handsome mortal, a prince no doubt," said one of them.

"You must be favoured by the gods if you succeeded in reaching us. Have you come to talk to us about the sunlit world above?"

"I came to ask for help," admitted Perseus. "I've been set the task of slaying Medusa. I believe you can help me."

"We are duty-bound to assist anyone who asks for our help," replied the youngest. "We have useful gifts for facing the gorgon."

She held out both arms and a leather bag appeared in them. "You will need this to contain Medusa's head once you have chopped it off. No other bag will hold it, for the gorgon's blood burns through everything."

"But he will not succeed in cutting off Medusa's head unless he wears this," added the second nymph. She plucked a helmet out of thin air. "Wear this when you approach the gorgons' lair, and you will be invisible."

"I have no gift to offer," said the third nymph as Perseus took the leather bag and the helmet of invisibility, "but I do have some words of advice. When you approach the gorgons' lair do so with courage. It is only with courage that you will get safely through your adventure…"

Face to Face with Medusa

The gorgons lived in a cave deep at the bottom of a mountain. The further Perseus travelled, the more barren the world had become. Grassy countryside gave way to rocky plains and sandy desert. The sparkling blue sea had turned into a deep, jet-black ocean, its waves forever pounding against sheer cliffs.

Now he was fluttering down at the mouth of the cave. The entrance was half-blocked with a mountain of boulders. Flying closer, he realized they were not rocks at all; they were people and animals, all turned to stone.

Perseus put on the helmet of invisibility. This was surely the gorgons' lair. There was a terrible stench of rotting meat. Perseus listened. There was someone on the other side of the boulders. He could hear sniggering, and the smacking of lips.

"A very good dinner, Euryale," said a shrill voice. "Very tasty indeed."

"Why, thank you, Stheno," replied a second voice, just as shrill. "I like a good piece of raw meat for my supper."

"I do hope Medusa comes home soon," continued the first voice. "It's getting late. She must be very hungry."

"Her snakes must be ravenous too," added the second voice. "Oh, here she is now."

Perseus heard the beating of wings behind him, accompanied by the angry hiss of snakes. He put his hands over his eyes and didn't take them off until he could hear all three gorgons talking again.

"Where did you go, Medusa? Did you turn anyone to stone?"

The only answer was a grunt. There was a long pause as Medusa ate her dinner, the snakes on her head hissing for titbits. Then the light in the cave was doused. Perseus waited until he could hear the gorgons snoring.

He held up Athena's shield and slowly entered the cave. Medusa's reflection in the shield looked hideous. Even in sleep, the face was angry. The snakes on the gorgon's head hissed, their tongues flicked sleepily.

Perseus drew his adamant dagger. "Athena, Hermes, be with me," he prayed, and then he swooped down on Medusa, his eyes still fixed on her reflection in the shield. The snakes heard him coming and hissed alarmingly. The gorgon's eyes flew open, her bronze claws lashed out, but it was too late! The adamant dagger sliced through the air and a second later Medusa's head was rolling across the cave floor.

Perseus reached out to grab it, his eyes still fixed firmly on its reflection in the shield. He grasped it firmly by the writhing snakes, which tried to bite him, and thrust it into his hunting bag. The other two gorgons, awoken by the snakes' hissing, leapt up and screeched angrily, the snakes on their heads spitting poison in every direction. They peered about them, but they could not see Perseus because he was still wearing the helmet of invisibility.

He speedily darted out of the cave, thanking the gods for his victory.

The Princess on the Rock

Perseus soared through the cobalt sky, the hunting bag with Medusa's head bumping against his hip. He was half way home to Seriphos.

Below him the sea sparkled. He was skimming along the coast of Africa, the shore outlined with trees and beaches and, sometimes, walled cities overlooking ship-filled harbours.

It was early afternoon and everyone in the world seemed to be indoors, sheltering from the scorching sun. Everyone except one lone figure, seemingly asleep on a smooth rock below.

Perseus swooped down for a closer look. He was amazed to discover it was a young woman. A very beautiful young woman. She was chained to the rock and unable to escape!

"Greetings!" said Perseus as he landed on the rock.

"Greetings to you, sir," she replied, obviously surprised by the sight of a stranger dropping out of the sky.

Perseus smiled. "Why are you chained to this rock? Have you been caught stealing and condemned to die?"

"I am not a thief," said the young woman. "My name is Andromeda. I am a princess, the daughter of Cepheus, the king of Joppa and his wife Queen Cassiopeia. My mother insulted the god Poseidon by claiming she was more beautiful than any of his nymphs. He sent a terrible sea monster to ravage our city. My father consulted an oracle and it told him to offer me as sacrifice. Any moment now, the sea monster will rise out of the waves to devour me."

"Your Highness," said Perseus, who had fallen in love with Andromeda the moment she had opened her mouth to speak, "I cannot let you perish at the hands of a terrible sea monster. I am of noble blood too, and know how to use a sword and dagger."

Hope flickered in Andromeda's eyes and she smiled. "Do you think you can save me?"

"I will do more than save you," replied Perseus. "I will take you away with me and, if you are willing, I shall make you my queen."

Andromeda's smile grew even wider. "If you do indeed save our city from this monster, I am sure my father would give you my hand in marriage," she said. "I will gladly marry you, for it is the gods themselves that have brought us together and I admire your bravery."

As the sun started to set, the sea turned a warm gold, the sky a soft coral. Perseus felt a rumble under his feet. The rock they were on began to tremble furiously. Perseus stood up in alarm, and shielded his eyes with his hands while he looked out to sea. The surface of the water was starting to hiss and bubble, as if a great fire had been lit underneath. Dolphins leapt up in alarm and the shoreline became alive with crabs fleeing the water.

Then a great wave splashed on to the shore, nearly knocking Perseus off his feet, and the head of a giant sea monster rose steadily out of the sea.

What a hideous creature it was! A giant serpent covered in bronze scales! It had a pair of large claws with razor-sharp nails. Its eyes, red as live coals, were small and full of anger. The monster half-rose out of the water and roared, spraying the shore with white-hot steam. Its mouth was full of pointed teeth, each one as sharp as a dagger. The creature looked round and then fixed its eyes on Andromeda.

Perseus dived up into the air, the wings on his sandals whirring loudly. He drew his adamant dagger and called out, "Come after me first, you beast! Slay the hero before the damsel."

The serpent turned to face him and roared again. Perseus swooped down at it, aiming for the neck. The monster's tongue flicked out of its mouth and the dagger went flying through the air, falling on to the rock right next to Andromeda.

Now the monster lunged forward, grabbing Perseus' right foot in its mouth. Andromeda screamed out in alarm. Perseus tried to reach for the bag at his hip. He managed to jab the cord to open it, shut his eyes and quickly whipped out Medusa's head.

"Look on this, serpent."

The serpent let go of his foot immediately. Its red eyes blazed with fury then grew dull as they settled on Medusa's horrifying face. It opened its mouth to roar again but the sound died in its throat. It had been turned to stone!

A Present for King Polydectes

"Where is my mother?" Perseus had returned to Seriphos, leaving Andromeda to prepare for their wedding at her father's palace.

Dictys clasped him round the shoulder. "She is living with the priestesses in Athena's temple. She did not dare stay here after you left. Polydectes was so sure Medusa would kill you, he swore to make her his queen again right away. That's why I sent her to the temple. No man, not even a king, would dare enter its sacred grounds."

"Where is Polydectes now?" demanded Perseus.

"He is having a banquet at his palace. I think he is announcing his wedding to your mother after the meal."

"If he is having a wedding, it is only right I take him a gift," said Perseus. He flew in his sandals to Athena's temple and hovered over the courtyard. Below him, a cluster of women were sitting at the looms, weaving tapestries.

"Mother," called Perseus.

Danae looked up from her work and her face lit up when she saw her son. "I cannot come down, mother, for it is forbidden for men to step inside Athena's temple. I just wanted you to know I am back, safe and sound, and I shall rid you of Polydectes before the sun rises."

Danae nodded, tears of joy streaming down her face. Perseus flew to King Polydectes' palace. The banquet had already started. He could hear music and a poet singing. The smell of roast boar wafted out of the open doors.

Perseus came to ground in the courtyard. He trotted up the steps and pushed the curtains aside. All the guests gasped. King Polydectes looked up from his wine cup.

"Why, Perseus," he said, with a smirk. "You have survived your encounter with Medusa."

"Yes, indeed," replied Perseus.

"Ah, but have you really brought me my wedding gift?" said the king. He looked round the hall, his eyes blazing with malice. "Or have you made up a story to impress the ladies with your prowess?"

"I have conquered the gorgon Medusa," replied Perseus. "Her head is here, in my bag."

King Polydectes started laughing, and the men in the hall laughed too.

"Did you hear that?" he roared. "The young hero tracked down the elusive Medusa and chopped off her head."

"No doubt the head belongs to a sheep or a young boar," laughed King Polydectes.

"If you do not believe me, see for yourself," said Perseus. He looked round the guests in the hall. "If you are my friends, shield your eyes." Most of the men closed their eyes. Perseus opened the bag, closed his eyes and drew out Medusa's head.

King Polydectes had only a moment to notice the purple eyes of the gorgon, the green scaly skin, the mass of snakes on her head…then the wine cup slipped from his hand and fell to the marble floor.

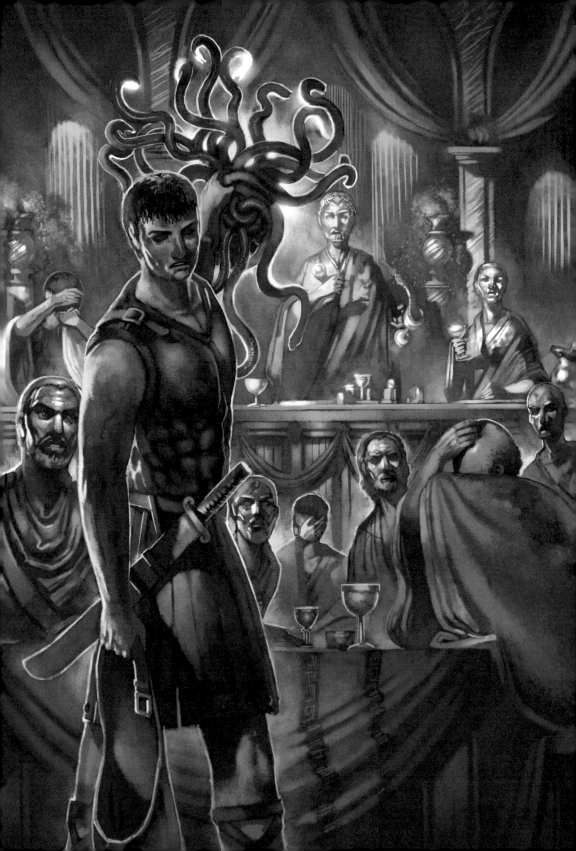

A New King

With Polydectes turned to stone, his brother Dictys became king of Seriphos. The fisherman lacked the manners of his brother but he more than made up for them with kindness and loyalty to his subjects. His wife and Queen Danae came to live in the palace, Queen Danae happy to be safe at last.

Perseus and Andromeda married in the city of Joppa. King Cepheus offered Perseus the throne but the young man turned it down.

He wanted to return to Argos, the city he had left as a baby in a wooden chest. His mother had told him all about his grandfather Acrisius and what the oracle had predicted. He bore the old king no grudge. Who, threatened by the fear of death, would not do anything in their power to survive?

He journeyed to Argos in his winged sandals, only to find his grandfather had travelled to the kingdom of Larissa to watch the games. He flew there himself, arriving as the games were in full swing.

A discus-throwing contest was about to start as he entered the stadium. "Will you take part, stranger?" asked a man. "The prize is a laurel wreath and your name carved on a monument in the city square."

Perseus accepted the challenge. It had been years since he had hurled a discus but he was sure he could hold his own against the local sportsmen.

The game started. One by one, the young men threw their discus, earning applause or ridicule from the spectators.

Soon it was Perseus' turn. He grasped the discus in his right hand, ground his right heel in the sand and swung round on his hips.

The discus flew out of his grasp, rising high in the air. He was hoping it would land at the other end of the ground, earning him the prize, but it was not to be. The discus landed in the crowds, hitting one of the spectators.

The old man keeled over. Dead! It was King Acrisius. The oracle had been right, the old ruler was killed by his grandson.

Perseus inherited the throne of Argos. His mission over, he returned to Seriphos and placed the gifts from the gods under the oak tree. One by one, they disappeared: the helmet of invisibility, the winged sandals, the adamant dagger and the hunter's bag containing Medusa's head. Soon there were was only Athena's shield left.

An owl hooted in the tree. Then Athena appeared, her face shining with light.

"Well done, Perseus," she said. "You have rid the world of Medusa, saved Andromeda from the sea monster, and made Dictys king of Seriphos."

She smiled. "Good things happen when heroes set forth on adventure." She held up the shield for Perseus to see. An image of Medusa's face had appeared on it, etched in the bronze in fine lines.

"From now on," said the goddess, "the look of Medusa will not harm. Instead it will protect anyone who looks upon it and prays to me."

ITALY

IONIAN
SEA

Larissa ⑦

GREECE

SICILY

Argos ⑥

MEDITERRANEAN
SEA

Nymphs of
the underworld

③

② Grey Sisters

N

LIBYA

BULGARIA

The
Ancient Greek World

Perseus' journey.....
Places visited.......... ❶

GEAN
EA

TURKEY

Seriphos

④

Gorgons' Lair

CYPRUS

⑤

Andromeda's
Rock

EGYPT

Family Tree

- **CHRONOS**
  - **HERA**
  - **ZEUS**
    - **HERMES** *(mother: Maia)*
      - **PERSEUS** *(mother: Queen Danae)* — **PRINCESS ANDROMEDA**
        - **KING STHENELUS** — NICIPPE
          - **KING EURYSTHEUS**
    - **ATHENA** *(mother: Metis)*
    - **ARTEMIS** *(mother: Leto)*
    - **APOLLO** *(mother: Leto)*
      - **HERCULES** *(mother: Queen Alcmene)*
  - **POSEIDON**
  - **HADES**
    - **TANTALUS** *(mother: Pluto)*
      - **KING PELOPS**
        - **KING PITTHEUS** *(mother: Hippodameia)*
          - **PRINCESS AETHRA** — **KING AEGEUS**
            - **THESEUS**
    - **DIONYSUS** *(mother: Senele)*
    - **MAGNES** *(mother: Thyia)*
      - **KING POLYDECTES**
      - **DICTYS**
- **HYPERION** — **THEIA**
  - **KING AIETES** — EID
    - **PRINCESS MEDEA**
  - **KING AESON** — **QUEEN ALCIMEDE**
    - **JASON**

KEY

TITAN   **GOD**   **GODDESS**   **HERO**   **KING**   **QUEEN**   **PRINCESS**

Editor: Tasha Percy
Designer: Martin Taylor
Editorial Director: Victoria Garrard
Art Director: Laura Roberts-Jensen

Copyright © QED Publishing 2014

First published in the UK in 2014 by
QED Publishing, A Quarto Group company,
The Old Brewery, 6 Blundell Street, London N7 9BH
www.qed-publishing.co.uk

All rights reserved. No part of this publication may be reproduced, stored in a retrieval system,
or transmitted in any form or by any means, electronic, mechanical, photocopying,
recording, or otherwise, without the prior permission of the publisher, nor be otherwise
circulated in any form of binding or cover other than that in which it is published and
without a similar condition being imposed on the subsequent purchaser.

A catalogue record for this book is available from the British Library.

ISBN 978 1 78171 638 0

Printed in China